FAIR PLAY OR FOUL?

ALAN DURANT

ILLUSTRATED BY
CHRIS SMEDLEY

MACMILLAN CHILDREN'S BOOKS

First published 1998 by Macmillan Children's Books
a division of Macmillan Publishers Limited
25 Eccleston Place, London SW1W 9NF
Basingstoke and Oxford
www.macmillan.co.uk

Associated companies throughout the world

ISBN 0 330 35127 3

3 5 7 9 8 6 4

A CIP catalogue record for this book is available from
the British Library.

Typeset in Baskerville BE
Printed and bound in Great Britain by Mackays of Chatham plc, Kent

Titles in the **Leggs United** series

All **Leggs United** titles can be ordered at your local bookshop or are available by post from Book Service by Post (tel: 01624 675137).

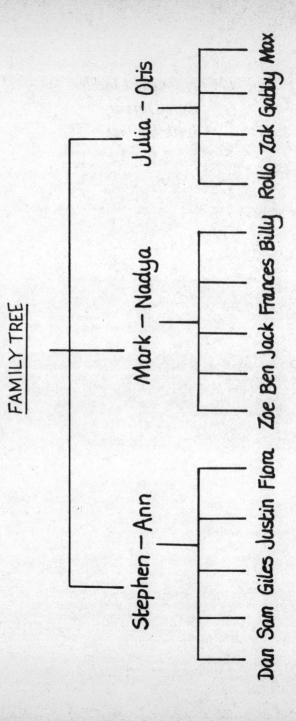

For my toughest tackler,
Amy Durant,
with big love

Chapter One
SOFT AS BUTTER

"**O**w!" Dan cried, hopping up and down in pain.

"Sorry, mate," said the Downside attacker who'd just kicked him on the shin. "I was going for the ball."

Dan grimaced and rubbed his sore leg. "Going for the ball!" he exclaimed. "You weren't even close." He shook his head in disgust.

"Are you OK, Dan?" asked Giles, one of Dan's younger twin brothers. "Is your leg broken?"

"You look really white," said Justin, the other twin.

"Like a ghost," Giles added.

"Yeah, like Archie," Justin confirmed. At the mention of their ghostly relative, the twins glanced across at the touchline.

The late Archibald Legg, former inside forward and star of Muddington Rovers, now the phantom manager of Leggs United, was in his usual match pose. He stood very straight with his hands on his hips, one foot on the old ball which, for over sixty years, had been his home. He was dressed, as ever, in an ancient Muddington Rovers strip with thick shin-pads and clumpy leather football boots. The paleness of his skin contrasted with the bright red of his big caterpillar eyebrows, enormous walrus moustache and fiery shock of hair. Around him there was a strange ghostly shimmer that blurred his outline.

At this particular moment Archie's face bore a hugely contented smile. Leggs United, the team he had formed during the summer from the children of three related families – two sets of Leggs and their cousins, the Brownes – were 3–1 up in their opening game of the season. It was also their first match ever in the Muddington

Junior League, a local football league for under-twelves.

Archie couldn't have hoped for a better start. His tactics had worked to perfection. The Leggs United score could easily have been doubled if the post and the bar hadn't come to Downside's rescue. As it was, goals by Sam, Zak and Ben had put Leggs United in a comfortable position. Downside's goal had been no more than a late consolation.

The full-time whistle blew and Archie nodded with satisfaction.

"Well played, team," he congratulated his players as they walked off the pitch. Dan was the last to leave, hobbling behind his younger sister Sam and his cousin and best friend Zak Browne.

"Well done, laddy," Archie greeted him. "You played a true captain's part."

"Yes, and I've got the bruises to show for it," Dan grumbled. His round face bore a pained expression.

"A few bruises never hurt," declared Archie, his moustache bristling. "Why, I often used to finish a match black and blue. It's a man's game, you know."

Sam humphed indignantly and flicked her fringe back.

"Well, you know what I mean," Archie added hastily. "Of course," he continued, "football was tougher in my day. The ball was much heavier and the boots were a lot harder." He glanced down at his own polished steel toecaps. "If you got a kick on the ankle from one of those you knew it all right. Why, I remember . . ."

Archie was fond of talking. After spending over half a century in Dan and Sam's loft, trapped inside an old football with no one to talk to, he was eager to make up for lost time. From the moment he'd fizzed out of the old ball like a genie from a magic lamp, he'd made a huge impression on his young relatives. He loved telling them what football was like in his day and, most of the time, they loved to listen. Right now, though, Dan wasn't in the mood for listening to stories. He just wanted to go inside and rest his bad leg, then go home and lie in a nice, hot bath. When Archie paused for an instant, he quickly seized his opportunity.

"Mum and Dad are waiting. I think we'd better go and get changed," he said. "Come on, Sam, Zak."

He picked up the old ball and started limping away.

"Soft as butter," tutted Archie and he raised his bushy eyebrows dismissively. Then, his ghostly size-twelve boots hovering above the ground, the phantom footballer glided across the grass towards the changing rooms.

Chapter Two
LEGS AND
NO LEGS

Dan's leg was still sore next morning. There was a big brown and yellow bruise on his shin. He showed it to Sam at breakfast.

"Eugh," she said. "It looks like a mouldy banana."

"Sounds nasty," said their dad, Dr Stephen Legg, pouring himself a cup of tea. He peered at Dan's leg. "You ought to wear shin-pads, you know."

"I will in future," said Dan ruefully.

Sam pulled a face. "I don't like shin-pads," she said. "They slow you down and they're uncomfortable."

Stephen Legg laughed and shook his head. "You think they're uncomfortable *nowadays*," he said. He went over to the kitchen dresser, opened one of the doors and took something out. "Take a look at these," he said. "I found them in a junk shop the other day."

Ann Legg looked up from her newspaper. "Not more junk," she sighed. It was while clearing out junk earlier in the summer, that the Leggs had discovered the old football haunted by Archie.

Dan and Sam stared at the objects on the table in front of them.

"What are they, Dad?" Sam asked.

Dan picked up one of the objects and studied it. It was shaped a bit like a cowboy's gun holster. The front was made of grooved leather, the kind he had sometimes seen on the seats of old cars in Legg's Motors, his uncle Mark's garage. The back was flat and stiff. The thing itself was quite thick, though, so it must have been stuffed with something. It was surprisingly heavy too.

"Is it an old shin-pad?" Dan said at last, pulling at one of his ears.

"It is," his dad confirmed with a nod of his large, bearded face. "Imagine playing with those under your socks. They'd slow you down all right."

"These must be like the ones Archie wore when he played," Dan said. "No wonder he didn't care about getting kicked. I reckon you'd break your toe if you kicked one of these."

"Yeah," Sam agreed. She screwed up her freckly nose. "How could anyone play football in those?"

"Why don't you ask Archie?" suggested Stephen Legg.

"Good idea," said Dan. "Come on, Sam." He picked up the old shin-pads and they went off into the sitting room to call up Archie from the old football.

The ball was now kept in a glass-fronted cabinet, on top of which was a framed photograph of Archie in his playing days, before he'd been struck down by a bolt of lightning. Dan gazed at the photo while Sam took the ball out of the cabinet and started to rub it gently. Then, as if she were Aladdin summoning the genie, she wailed, "Archie. Arise, O Archie!"

Barely a second later, Archie was there. He leapt out of the ball in a quivery fizz and loomed over the children, shimmering. It was a dramatic entrance, but Dan and Sam hardly batted an eyelid. They were used to Archie now.

Archie's face had a satisfied glow about it. But something wasn't right.

"Archie," Sam giggled. "Where are your legs?"

The phantom footballer glanced down at his bottom half. His eyes widened as he discovered it wasn't there.

"Mmm," he mused, his bushy eyebrows twitching curiously. "It appears that I am a Legg without legs. And Archibald Legg without legs is like bacon without eggs. Hold on one moment." Archie narrowed his eyes, gazing fixedly at the TV and video to draw electricity into his ghostly figure. Electricity, he'd discovered, gave him strength and energy. He screwed up his face so tightly that his eyebrows and moustache almost met in one great red hairy embrace.

Suddenly, the room seemed to crackle with

electricity. Archie's hair stood up on end as if he'd just had an electric shock. He looked as if he was on fire. Sam and Dan shielded their eyes, dazzled.

After a few moments, the fieriness faded and Archie became clear once more. And now, the children noted, he was complete. Archie registered this fact as well.

"Ah, that's better," he said happily. "Just a small energy problem, nothing to worry about." He sighed contentedly. "Now, how can I assist you?" he asked.

"We wanted to show you these," Dan said. He held out the old shin-pads for Archie to see. Archie's face lit up at once.

"Shin-guards!" he exclaimed. "Excellent, excellent." He took the shin-pads in his hands and gazed at them lovingly. "See how beautifully made they are – just like my own." He glanced down at the large bulge beneath each of his socks.

"They're made of leather, aren't they?" Dan said.

"Indeed they are," Archie enthused. "Very fine leather at that – and lined with wool. You wouldn't suffer sore shins with these on."

"I couldn't play in those," Sam sniffed, tossing back her head. "They're much too heavy. I wouldn't be able to move fast enough."

"Ah, you'd be surprised," said Archie. "Cliff Bastin managed well enough. A faster winger you're never likely to see." The phantom footballer's face took on the warm, respectful expression that it always had when he talked about the Arsenal team of the 1930s or its manager, the great Herbert Chapman. "But, of course," he continued, "it's not how fast you run that's really important. It's how fast you think." He drew himself up proudly. "And, though I say it myself," he added with a twitch of his moustache, "no one thought faster than me."

The two children raised their eyes and sighed.

"The game wasn't as fast in your day, though, was it?" said Dan. "That's what the experts say."

"Oh, do they?" Archie bristled. "Do they indeed? Well I'll tell you, it was a lot harder. If you didn't wear shin-guards, you wouldn't last a day."

"Things are different now," Sam insisted.

"Indeed they are," Archie agreed. "More's the pity. In my day . . ."

His lecture was cut short by an excited exclamation from Dan. "Do you know what, Archie?" he cried. "You should come with us and watch Muddington Rovers play! Then you'd see what football today is really like." His round face beamed with enthusiasm.

Archie looked pleased too. "What an excellent idea," he said. "I should like to see my old team in action again." He nodded contentedly. "I'm sure I could teach them a thing or two . . ."

Chapter Three
ARCHIE SEES RED

Archie was amazed by how much things had changed at Muddington Rovers since his day. For a start, there was the programme. In his time, he said, it had just been a couple of sheets of paper, printed in black and white, costing one penny. His eyes nearly popped out of his head when he saw the present-day, full-colour item – and heard the price.

"£2! For a programme!" he exclaimed. "Why, that's daylight robbery!"

"It is a lot, I agree with you," said Stephen Legg. "Mind you, it's even worse in the Premier League." Muddington Rovers were currently in the second division, having been relegated the season before. When Archie had been a player, the club had been in the top division.

The ground had changed a lot too. The old terraces, on which the crowds had stood to watch matches, had been replaced by seating. There were stands now on all four sides of the pitch. Archie didn't approve. He glared at the rows of seats, many of which were empty, with bristling disdain.

"It may be more comfortable," he sniffed, "but where's the atmosphere? When I played here, the ground was full to the rafters every game. You could hear the tension and excitement in the crowd as you ran on to the pitch."

"Well, the crowd isn't very big today," Dan admitted. "But you'll still hear a roar when the teams come out." He cast a sly glance at Sam, who was sitting the other side of the phantom footballer. "Sam will shriek her head off when she sees Tommy Banks," he said teasingly. "She always does."

Sam's cheeks went as red as her hair. She glowered at her brother. "Of course I cheer when I see him," she said defensively. "He's a great player."

Just moments later, Muddington Rovers arrived on the pitch in their black and green striped shirts. The five children who'd come with Stephen Legg and Archie to the match – Sam, Dan, their cousin Zak, and the twins, Giles and Justin – leapt up excitedly, shouting and clapping with the rest of the crowd. Archie, meanwhile, looked on with quiet interest.

Sam pointed to a shortish, chunky player with spiky blond hair and a small goatee beard. "That's Tommy Banks," she told Archie.

Her ghostly ancestor looked unimpressed. "He seems a bit tubby for a footballer," he remarked with a critical wrinkle of his walrus moustache.

"Wait till you see him play," Sam enthused. "He's the best." She gazed ardently at her footballing hero.

"Yeah, Tommy Banks is cool," said Zak, nodding his head in a waft of black ringlets.

"He's OK," said Dan casually. He glanced at Sam again out of the corner of his eye and she stuck her tongue out at him.

"Now, now," said Archie soothingly. "We're all on the same side."

The game kicked off and Muddington Rovers quickly went on the attack. For the first five minutes, Easthampton, Muddington's opponents, hardly touched the ball. The play was all in the Easthampton half. Tommy Banks was brilliant. He made one chance for his fellow striker, Dean Jones, then had a great shot himself that was saved spectacularly by the keeper.

"See," said Sam, turning to Archie, "I told you he was good, didn't I?"

"Mmm," Archie murmured appreciatively. "He reminds me a little of Alex James, the great Arsenal playmaker."

Sam grinned; this, from Archie, was praise indeed.

Muddington Rovers continued to dominate the game. They had all the play, but just couldn't score the goal they deserved. Dean Jones missed another good chance and Tommy Banks hit the post with a curling free kick from the edge of the penalty area. The crowd groaned with disappointment.

But at last the goal came and, to Sam's particular delight, it was Tommy Banks who scored. He played a clever one-two with Dean Jones, burst past a defender and slotted the ball calmly into the corner of the net.

Once more the crowd stood and cheered. Stephen Legg waved his programme in the air like a flag. Sam, Dan and Zak hugged one another. Giles and Justin smacked hands in a high five. Even Archie was excited. He raised his hands in the air and glowed brightly surrounded by a fiery aura.

At half-time the score was still 1–0.

"Well, Archie, how are the team shaping up, do you think?" Stephen Legg inquired amiably.

Archie stroked his moustache thoughtfully. "They are doing quite well," he said. "But they should have scored more goals." He pursed his lips in a gesture of dissatisfaction. "They need more than two attackers, I should say." Archie favoured the WM formation – a system of playing made popular by Herbert Chapman – with three, sometimes four strikers.

"At least they're winning," said Dan, who was relieved that the Muddington defence hadn't let in any goals for once.

However, this state of affairs didn't last long. Two minutes into the second half, Easthampton equalized with just about their first real attack of the match. A long clearance found the lone Easthampton striker unmarked with only the goalkeeper to beat, which he did quite easily – *too* easily, in fact, according to Archie.

"I could have saved that with my eyes closed," he seethed. No one contradicted him. The children all knew what a good goalkeeper he was. At the end of most Leggs United training sessions he went in goal and no one could score against him.

"I think he did have his eyes closed – that was the problem," Stephen Legg remarked drily.

After Easthampton's early goal, the match became much more evenly balanced. It was also far more competitive than in the first half, with lots of hard tackles, many of which the referee penalized as fouls – greatly to Archie's disgust.

"What's the matter with this referee?" he complained after the whistle had gone for yet another foul. "There was nothing wrong with that challenge."

"You're not allowed to tackle from behind," Dan said.

"But the defender got the ball," Archie protested.

"It doesn't matter," said Zak, who was the family expert on football rules and facts. "If you tackle from behind and you bring down your opponent, it's a foul."

"What poppycock!" exclaimed Archie, outraged. "In my day that would have been applauded as an excellent tackle."

Archie was even more upset when, a moment later, the referee booked the defender who'd made the "foul" tackle. He booked six more during the second half – all quite unfairly, in Archie's opinion. Each time the referee reached for his yellow card, Archie threw up his hands and groaned in dismay. "Defenders wouldn't have lasted two minutes in my day with this lily-livered, whistle-happy ref," he moaned.

It was the final booking of the game that stirred up Archie's fiercest indignation. It came very near the end of the match. Muddington Rovers were attacking, making a final push for the winning goal. A high cross was sent over from the wing, right into the goalmouth. The Easthampton goalkeeper leapt to catch the ball and, as he did so, Dean Jones barged into him, knocking ball and goalie into the net. Archie was on his feet at once, arms raised in jubilation.

"Goal!" he cried and he danced a little jig to celebrate. Then he turned to the others with a huge, hairy grin. "We've won," he declared.

The children laughed. The twins laughed so much they fell off their seats.

"That wasn't a goal, Archie," said Dan.

"He fouled the goalie," said Sam.

"Barging the goalie is against the rules," Zak confirmed.

Archie stared at them for an instant in disbelief. Then he turned back to the pitch and saw that the referee had indeed blown his whistle, not for a goal, but for a free-kick. Not only that, but he was writing Dean Jones' name in his notebook.

Archie saw red. In a flash he whooshed down the aisle between the rows of seats to the edge of the pitch, shaking his fists at the referee and shouting.

"Numbskull! Half-wit! Blind, bald-headed coot!" he screamed.

Archie's outburst, however, was in vain. As the Legg family had already discovered, only they could see and hear Archie; to everyone else he was quite invisible and inaudible. At this particular moment, that was probably a very good thing, Dan thought, as he watched his ghostly ancestor ranting and raving like a madman, his outline ablaze with anger. No, the world definitely wasn't ready for Archie, Dan decided. He was best kept in the family.

Chapter Four
TACKLING PRACTICE

Archie was intrigued but not hugely impressed by his first glimpse of modern-day professional football. The game was faster, he admitted, but he didn't think it was as skilful as in his day. It wasn't nearly as tough either. When he was playing, he said, it was perfectly legal to shoulder-charge the goalkeeper. He'd seen many goals scored that way.

"Football's supposed to be a physical game," Archie stated. Then he told his relatives about a 1934 match between England and Italy, known as the "Battle of Highbury". Seven Arsenal players were in the England team, including the centre forward, Ted Drake. The battle started when he broke the toe of an Italian defender in a tackle. The Italians went mad and retaliated by trying to kick England off the pitch. By the end of the game, nearly all the England players were injured: one had a broken nose, another a broken arm, another an injured ankle, another a cut leg . . .

"But they won," Archie said proudly. "It was a great victory. They didn't hide behind the referee's whistle – they got on with the game like men."

"It sounds more like war than football," Dan remarked.

"Yeah," said Sam. "Girls don't foul like that. We play properly."

"So do boys," said Zak.

"Yes," Dan agreed. "And we tackle too – which is more than you do, Sam."

Before Sam could retort, Archie raised his hand in the air. "As I said before," he boomed, "we're all on the same side here. Save your battling for the opposition on the pitch."

Unlike the older children, the twins thought Archie's story was brilliant. When they got home, they acted out their own Battle of Highbury in the hall. They made such a row that, after a while, Ann Legg appeared with a red card and ordered them both off to bed.

At the next Leggs United training session, Archie concentrated on defensive skills – especially tackling.

"Oh, not tackling," Sam groaned. Everyone knew that Sam thought tackling was boring.

Archie gave her a stern glare. "Tackling is of vital importance," he declared. "If you do not have the ball, you cannot play." He wrinkled his big moustache. "That is a lesson Muddington Rovers would do well to learn," he said. "In particular, that chubby fellow you are so fond of – Piggy Banks, wasn't it?"

"Piggy Banks! Piggy Banks!" repeated the twins and everyone laughed – except Sam. She pushed back her fringe and scowled at Archie.

"His name's *Tommy* Banks," she said fiercely, "and he's not chubby."

"Mmm, well," Archie murmured. "He could do with improving his tackling anyway."

For the tackling practice, Archie paired

everyone up. One player was an attacker and one a defender. The defender had to get the ball off the attacker. Then they swapped round. Sam was partnered with Dan. He was the best tackler in the team and he got the ball off Sam quite easily. But she couldn't get the ball off him – not that she tried very hard.

"You're too big," she complained bitterly. Dan was a good head taller than his sister and he was a lot broader.

"The bigger they are, the harder they fall," Archie commented, hands on hips. "Tackling is as much about timing as strength. Make your tackle at the right moment and you take the ball; time your tackle wrongly and you get nothing – except perhaps a bruise . . . or a booking." He frowned disapprovingly, remembering the Muddington Rovers match. "Allow me to demonstrate."

Archie got Sam to run at him with the ball three times. The first time he lunged at the ball before Sam had reached him and she easily sidestepped the tackle. The second time, Archie waited until Sam was almost past him before trying to tackle, and once again

Sam evaded him easily. The rest of the team cheered.

"Go for it, Sam!" Zak called. Sam wrinkled her small, freckly nose and grinned triumphantly. Then she prepared to take on Archie for a third time.

She rolled the ball in front of her, keeping it close to her feet, confident that she could beat her ghostly ancestor. She moved closer, swaying, waiting for the challenge . . . and whoomf! Suddenly, the ball was no longer there. She looked down in astonishment then turned to see Archie behind her with the ball at

his feet. It had all happened so fast and she hadn't felt a thing.

"Wow!" she said in deep admiration. "That was so quick."

"Cool!" Zak enthused.

"What a tackle! How did you do that?" Dan asked, equally amazed.

Archie waggled his moustache and glowed. "Practice, just practice," he said with a shrug. Then he raised one eyebrow. "Oh, and genius, of course," he added smugly.

Chapter Five

AN UNWELCOME VISITOR

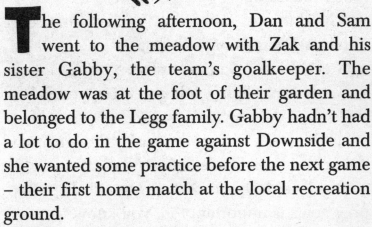

The following afternoon, Dan and Sam went to the meadow with Zak and his sister Gabby, the team's goalkeeper. The meadow was at the foot of their garden and belonged to the Legg family. Gabby hadn't had a lot to do in the game against Downside and she wanted some practice before the next game – their first home match at the local recreation ground.

"I need some proper practice too," Sam declared, "after all that *tackling* yesterday." She darted a sharp glance at Dan. "Let's do some shooting," she said.

"We could have a competition," Zak suggested.

"Yes, good idea," Sam agreed quickly. She and Zak both looked at Dan.

"Suits me," Dan said nonchalantly.

For the next half hour or so, Sam, Dan and Zak took it in turns to fire shots at Gabby, keeping count of the goals they managed to score. Zak and Sam tied with eight goals each; Dan only had three.

"I'm a defender, not a striker," Dan reminded them.

"Good thing," said Sam. "You couldn't score if the goal was as big as a house."

"I got three," Dan protested.

"Only cos Gabby felt sorry for you," Sam jeered.

"He's good at *stopping* goals, though," said Zak, coming to Dan's defence.

"Yes," said Dan, nodding vigorously. "Stopping goals is important too, you know."

Sam tossed her head dismissively. "Huh," she humphed. Stopping goals, like tackling, was something she had no interest in.

Gabby had to go off to her gymnastics club,

so the other three children practised passing for a while. Then they sat down at the edge of the pitch to rest.

"Who are we playing next in the league?" asked Sam.

"Weldon Wanderers," said Zak.

Dan nodded. "I bet they'll be a lot tougher than Downside," he said.

"They couldn't be worse," Sam remarked.

"No, not unless they all had one leg," Dan laughed.

He looked up and the smile quickly vanished from his face, as he spotted a familiar, unwelcome figure peering at him over the fence. It was his arch-rival, Perry Nolan.

"What are you doing here?" Dan demanded coolly.

Perry pulled a face. "Just looking," he said. "No crime in that, is there?"

"Well, now you've looked, you can clear off," said Dan shortly.

Perry scowled. "You can't tell me what to do," he said. "I'm not one of your stupid team."

"We wouldn't have you," Sam said sharply. "We don't like cheats."

"No," said Dan. Earlier in the summer, when Leggs United had played Perry Nolan's team, Muddington Colts, in the Holt Nolan Football Challenge, Perry had dived outrageously to get a penalty. His dad, Holt Nolan, had been the referee. "You're just jealous cos we beat you," Dan jibed.

"You were lucky," said Perry. "Wait till we play you in the league."

"We'll just beat you again," said Dan defiantly.

"Yeah, wait till you come down to the rec," Sam added fierily. "You won't stand a chance."

Perry sneered. "Yeah?" he scoffed. "We thrashed Ledminster 8–0 last week. I got a hat-trick." Perry was always boasting about how good he was and how many goals he'd scored. It was one of the reasons why Dan disliked him so much.

"They must have been really useless," he sniped. "Or was your dad the ref again?"

"We beat Downside away," Zak said matter-of-factly.

"And on Saturday we're going to beat Weldon Wanderers," Sam added confidently.

This news had a dramatic effect on Perry. "Weldon Wanderers!" he exclaimed. "You're playing Weldon Wanderers on Saturday?"

"Yeah. What of it?" said Dan.

Perry's face broke into a huge gloating smile. "You'll see," he said, and he laughed. "You'd better get that lucky ball of yours – cos you're going to need it." He tapped his bike helmet. "You should get yourselves some of these too," he added. Then, still sniggering, he rode away on his bike, tooting his horn as he went.

"What do you think he meant?" Zak asked,

his large brown eyes looking unusually troubled.

"Oh, nothing," shrugged Dan. "He's just trying to wind us up, that's all. Ignore him."

"Yeah," said Sam swaggeringly. "We're not scared of anyone." Her face creased in a freckly grin. "We've got Archie, haven't we?"

Chapter Six
ARCHIE
SHOWS HOW

Over the next day or so, Perry Nolan's comments about Weldon Wanderers kept nagging at Dan. What had he meant exactly? *Why* would Leggs United need luck? *Why* would they need crash helmets? It was all rubbish probably, as he'd said at the time, but, well, what if there *was* something in what Perry had said? He should at least mention it to Archie, he decided.

At the next training session, Dan took Archie to one side. He spoke casually, as if he didn't really believe there was anything in Perry's talk – and he was quite relieved that Archie seemed to think the same.

"Sounds like a lot of poppycock," Archie scoffed with a flourish of his walrus moustache. "Besides, it's Leggs United that concerns me, laddy, not Weldon Wanderers." He eyed his captain with a steely gaze. "When I've finished with you," he intoned gravely, "you'll be more than a match for any team. Mark my words."

Archie was a good coach. He said it often enough himself – and, though they groaned when he did, his team agreed. Every one of them benefited from his skills training and tactical guidance.

He gave Gabby lots of shot practice – low shots into the corners especially, making her dive from side to side to improve her stretch. Herbert Chapman had done something similar with his goalkeeper, he explained.

As well as tackling techniques, he taught Dan and the twins about marking and covering. And he practised heading with Zak's brother, Rollo, who was the oldest and tallest player in the team.

"We need a target man at corners and free-kicks," Archie told him. "You could be our Ted Drake."

"But don't start any battles," joked Dan, who was standing nearby with Zak and Sam. Then the three of them laughed, because Rollo was the least aggressive person they knew. They'd never heard him raise his voice in anger, never mind get in a fight.

"Never mind the Battle of Highbury," sniffed Archie in disgust. "You're not even allowed to tackle properly these days."

The phantom coach set Sam and Zak a passing test, with two of the triplets, Ben and Frances, as their partners. They were both very fast runners and played on the wings.

In Archie's exercise, Ben had to kick the ball to Sam and then sprint forwards to get the return pass. Frances did the same with Zak. The real test for Sam and Zak was that they had to kick their passes over the top of a tall board that Archie had set up, and make the ball land just in front of the sprinting winger. If the pass was too far ahead or behind, or to one side, it was considered a failure.

To begin with, Sam and Zak failed a lot.

"This is too hard," Sam complained after ten minutes or so. "I'll never get it right."

"Rome wasn't built in a day," Archie remarked primly. "Practice makes perfect."

"You show us, then," Sam challenged her coach.

Archie wiggled his caterpillar eyebrows. "Very well," he said. He got Ben to kick the ball to him, then, glancing up, he placed the ball perfectly in the path of the speeding winger. Then he did the same thing on the other side with Frances. He turned to the cousins with a satisfied smile. All around his figure a hazy aura glowed.

"Cool!" said Zak admiringly.

"All right, you win," said Sam. Then she and Zak continued their practice – with increasing success.

With Zoe and Jack (the oldest of the triplets by two minutes), Archie worked mainly on balance and ball control. They were both reasonable players but were sometimes a little clumsy. In order to correct this, Archie marked out a line of large flowerpots and got the two children to weave in and out, keeping the ball close to their feet.

After a while, he moved the flowerpots closer together, then closer still . . . Then he set up a wooden plank above the ground, resting on the pots. Zoe and Jack had to move backwards and forwards across it, going faster each time.

Now and then, not surprisingly, one or the other fell off – but there wasn't far to fall. Once, Zoe lost her balance and dropped right on to Archie. Her glasses flew off and landed in his hair. Archie caught his young relative and lifted her high into the air for an instant, before placing her back on the plank again.

At that moment the postman happened to be passing the meadow. Glancing over the fence, he was astonished to see a girl and a pair of glasses floating in the air! It gave him such a shock that he crashed his bike into the fence. His mailbag fell off and letters scattered everywhere.

The children quickly ran to help him. Archie lent a hand too, picking up letters and returning them to the sack. But this only caused the poor postman more confusion – it looked to him as

if the letters were flying through the air by themselves! He blinked hard and shook his head.

"I'm not myself today, kids," he said with a dazed expression. Then, woozily, he got back on his bike and wobbled away up the road.

"He looks like he's seen a ghost," laughed Dan.

"Mmm," Archie murmured critically. "In my day, of course, postmen were made of much stronger stuff . . ."

Chapter Seven
PITCHING IN

At breakfast on Wednesday morning Stephen Legg had some bad news.

"Our pitch at the rec has fallen through," he told Sam and Dan gloomily. "It seems they double booked it by mistake. Another team had already reserved it."

"But can't we just play on one of the other pitches?" Dan asked.

Stephen Legg shook his head. "They're all booked," he said. "There are a few other places I could try, but I don't hold out much hope. It's very late now."

Dan tugged at his ear thoughtfully. "So what

happens if we can't get another pitch? Will we have to postpone the match?"

Stephen Legg sighed and ran his fingers through his beard. "I'm afraid not, Dan," he said sadly. "If we don't have a pitch by Saturday, then we have to concede the game to Weldon Wanderers."

"But that's not fair," Sam complained. "They win without having to play."

"It's in the league rules," Stephen Legg said mournfully.

Throughout the day, with increasing desperation, Stephen and Ann Legg phoned up parks and sports grounds in the area to try and find a new home ground for Leggs United. But by the end of the afternoon they had had no success. Everywhere was booked.

It was a very long-faced Sam who summoned Archie from the ball that evening. Next to her, Dan and Zak were looking equally miserable.

Oddly, however, their ghostly ancestor was not downcast at the children's news.

"Well, these things happen," he said calmly, with a twitch of his moustache. "It's of little matter."

The three children stared at him as if he were mad.

"Don't you understand, Archie?" Sam exclaimed. "If we don't have a pitch, then we can't play in the league."

Archie looked at Sam pitifully. "But we do have a pitch, laddy," he said. "Well, we have a ground, in any case."

"Where? What ground?" Dan quizzed his phantom relative.

Archie beamed. "Why, here, of course," he said. "The meadow."

"The meadow!" cried Sam.

"Cool," said Zak.

"But it's got no lines or goalposts or anything," Dan protested.

Archie waved a pale hand dismissively. "That's easily settled, laddy," he said lightly. "It just needs a bit of hard toil and teamwork."

"My dad'll help!" Zak cried with un-characteristic excitement. "I'll go and ask him now . . ."

Archie's suggestion was met with universal approval by his relatives. It was the obvious solution. The worry was whether the job could be completed in time. There were just two days to go before the Weldon match and there was lots to be done. Everyone would have to lend a hand – adults and children alike. Fortunately, the children were still on their summer holiday.

"It'll be great fun," Dan enthused. He couldn't wait to get started.

"Well, it'll be better than tackling practice, anyway," said Sam.

So it was agreed: the three families would spend the next couple of days trying to turn the meadow into a proper football pitch.

Next morning, the work began. Zak's father, Otis Browne, was a carpenter and he worked on building the goal frames. Ann Legg and Nadya Legg (the triplets' mother) were responsible for making the goal nets. Julia Browne's task was to make sure that the pitch was properly marked out and that the lines were all in their correct place. She borrowed a line-marker from Muddington Primary School where she was a teacher. Mark Legg supplied a motorized lawnmower from his garage, Legg's Motors, to cut the grass.

Stephen Legg was the only one of the parents

who didn't have a definite job. He wandered around, making lots of suggestions – most of which were quite impractical. Eventually, Ann Legg sent him off to inform the relevant people about Leggs United's change of ground.

"We don't want to do all this work and have no one turn up because they don't know where to come," she said.

"Very true," Stephen Legg agreed. "I'll go and phone the league secretary straight away."

The children all did their bit, too. Zak and Rollo helped their dad with building the goalposts and bar – and then painting them. Their little brother Max Browne, who was five, joined in as well. But he mainly painted himself. By the time the frame was finished, he was streaked all over in white paint.

"I think he's trying to look ghostly like his great-great-uncle Archie," laughed Otis Browne, shaking his head at the state of his youngest child.

"He looks more like a badger," said Zak.

"Or a skunk," suggested Rollo.

"Yeah – I'm a smelly skunk," said Max and,

going down on all fours, he chased his little cousin Flora across the meadow.

The job the children liked best was cutting the grass. They took it in turns to sit up next to Mark or Stephen Legg on the motor mower and trundle noisily across the meadow, churning up grass in their wake. Mark Legg let some of the older children – Dan, Sam and Zoe – have a go at driving the mower themselves. He showed them how to steer the mower so that it cut a straight strip of grass and then how to stop and turn the machine and how to change gear. There was only one nasty moment, when Sam took her hands off the steering wheel for a moment to wave to her mum and the mower veered to the left, bashing into the fence.

"Oh, well," shrugged Otis Browne, looking at the splintered fencing. "I needed to put a gate in the fence somewhere. I guess I'll just put it there."

Dan loved the mower – and so did Archie. He said it reminded him of the motor cars of his youth. Once, when Dan was driving, Archie rode along too. He stood at the back of the mower, radiant with pleasure, head held high – "like a king, surveying his kingdom", Stephen Legg said. And Dan reckoned that was right, because Archie's kingdom *was* the football pitch. That was where he reigned supreme. Not that Dan would tell his ghostly relative that – he was big-headed enough already!

The trickiest task was getting all the pitch measurements right and marking out the lines. Julia Browne's patience was sorely tested – particularly by the twins, Giles and Justin. They were supposed to be helping her by acting as

markers, but they kept getting distracted and running off to look at other things.

"Give me strength!" she exclaimed several times, as she looked up to see the other end of the tape measure wandering away over the meadow. Still, with the new school year less than a week away, trying to organize the twins was good preparation for what was to come, she said. Teaching her new class would be easy in comparison.

By Friday morning, the grass was all cut, but there was still a lot left to do.

"We'll never be ready," said Sam wearily, as she looked at the half of the pitch that still needed to be marked up.

"Yes, we will," Dan replied stirringly. "We've got to be." He ran over to help Julia with the line painting and, after a short rest, Sam joined him. They took over from the twins and immediately things started to move along faster.

By late Friday afternoon, the pitch was finished. All that remained was for the goals to be put up. Everyone was exhausted, but happy.

"We've done it," said Dan, looking with pride at the transformed meadow. "We've got a pitch."

"It looks great!" Sam confirmed, smiling broadly for the first time in two days. "Like a real football ground."

All the hard work, everyone agreed, had been worthwhile.

Archie was a little more critical. He gave the pitch a thorough inspection, pointing out a couple of places where the lines were a little bit blobby or not entirely straight. He found a few bumps too. But all in all, he appeared to be satisfied.

"Well, it's not exactly Highbury, but it will do," was his verdict. Then his serious expression relaxed into a glowing smile. "I believe Herbert Chapman would approve," he remarked contentedly.

Chapter Eight
BUTTERFLIES

Saturday was a fine day. The sun shone brightly in a blue, cloudless sky. Straight after breakfast Dan and Sam went to look at their new pitch. They passed the twins, Giles and Justin, who were racing snails on the lawn. It was hard to know which of the snails was winning, though, because they were going in opposite directions.

"You two," said Sam and she tapped her head to show that she thought they were completely mad. Then she followed Dan down to the meadow.

The goals were up now, with their nets. They gleamed white in the dewy sunshine. Dan and

Sam stood by the wall, taking in the scene before them and marvelling at how fresh and new it all looked.

"I'm glad we're playing here, rather than at the rec," Dan said dreamily. "It seems more special somehow." He tugged on his ear thoughtfully. "This really is *our* ground," he added proudly.

"Yes," said Sam. "And we're going to start with a win." She ran forward and banged a ball into one of the goals.

The morning really dragged, but at last lunchtime came, and after that, the countdown to the match at two o'clock. In that final hour before kick-off, Dan's stomach was filled with butterflies; he just couldn't wait for the game to start.

Archie had instructed Dan to gather the team together at quarter to two. As they assembled, Sam summoned the phantom manager from the old ball. He blazed out as if fired from a cannon.

"Right," he said, shimmering with energy, "I believe it is time for my team talk." He cast an approving eye over his players, crowded into the large sitting room of number 15 Poplar Street. They were all dressed in their smart team strip, which had been provided by Mark Legg. "I see we are ready to motor," he remarked playfully, nodding at the words *Legg's Motors* on the front of the team's shirts.

He coughed and his face took on a serious expression. "Now," he said gravely, his hairy eyebrows coming together in an upside down V, "this afternoon's game will be an historic occasion: the first ever competitive football match to be played at The Meadow, the new home ground of Leggs United." He paused momentarily before continuing: "To we Leggs – and Brownes – this is an event as momentous as the first ever Cup Final played at Wembley in 1923. Bolton beat West Ham by two goals to nil that day and one of the scorers was David Jack, who, as you know, was later signed by Herbert Chapman to play for Arsenal in that great forward line." Archie paused once more, shimmering with emotion, his eyes full of the awe they always held when he mentioned the great manager or his team. "This afternoon," he went on, his voice quivering with feeling, "I want you to play for me, as Arsenal played for Herbert Chapman."

Archie's words were met, at first, by total silence. His team were taken aback by the serious tone of his speech and not really sure how to react. Some of the younger members were quite bemused. It was Dan who finally found his tongue.

"Does that mean you want us to win?" he asked hesitantly.

Archie frowned. "Win?" he repeated, his whole body glowing. "Why, of course I want you to win, laddy. But winning's just part of the story. I want you to display the full range of skills and tactical brilliance that I, Archibald Legg, have taught you." He pursed his lips disapprovingly. "I would ask for some of the fighting spirit too," he sniffed, "but of course that is not part of the game nowadays, more is the pity."

"We may not fight, but we've got plenty of spirit," Sam protested. She turned to face the rest of the team. "Haven't we, Leggs United?"

"Yes!" came the loud and unanimous reply.

This response seemed to satisfy Archie. "Good, good," he said happily. Then, in one amazingly fluid movement, the phantom footballer dragged back the old ball with one foot, flicked it into the air and caught it on the end of his finger, where it span like a top. "Now, follow me to the pitch," he commanded. "I have something to show you."

Archie led his team down the garden, over the wall, and into the meadow. There they discovered Otis Browne, painting something behind one of the goals, with the line-marking whitewash. As Archie and the children approached, Otis gave a final dab with his brush and stood up straight. Dan, who was right behind Archie, was the first to see a kind of diagram, with a lot of lines and initials.

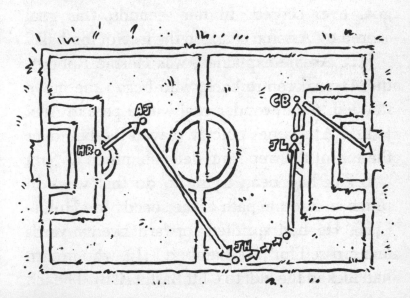

"There, all done," Otis murmured. He turned to Archie. "Is that how you wanted it, coach?" he enquired.

Archie put his hands on his hips and nodded. His face was rosy with contentment. "Excellent," he enthused. "Quite excellent."

"What is it?" asked Dan, who was standing right next to his ghostly relative now. The rest of the team were clustered around the curious painted diagram, studying it with a collective air of puzzlement.

"That," said Archie, wiggling his moustache theatrically, "is a picture of the most perfect goal ever scored. In ten seconds, this goal scored by Arsenal changed the face of football."

HR, Archie explained, was Herbie Roberts, the Arsenal centre back, who began the move that led to the wonder goal with a pass to Alex James (AJ). James quickly played the ball over the top of the opposing defence (much as Sam and Zak had been trying to do that week in practice) into the path of the speedy Joe Hulme (JH). He had sprinted forward twenty yards and crossed for Jack Lambert (JL), who in turn had flicked the ball to Cliff Bastin (CB). The left winger had wasted no time in banging the ball into the net.

"Nothing could be more perfect," Archie declared ecstatically, "and that is why I asked Otis to draw it here, right next to the pitch, where it will serve, I hope, as an inspiration to you all every time you set foot on this field." He looked around at his rather puzzled team with a serene expression.

As he was doing so, a tall figure dressed in black appeared at the meadow gate. "Looks like your ref's arrived. Someone had better go and open the gate," said Otis Browne sensibly.

At that moment, a packed mini-van drew into the road behind the meadow.

"Here's our opposition, too," Dan said and he had that butterflies-in-the-stomach feeling again – only now it felt as if the butterflies were all fluttering wildly. It was time, finally, for the game to begin.

Chapter Nine
NO PRISONERS

From the moment they marched into The Meadow, Dan had a bad feeling about Weldon Wanderers. For a start, they were all so big – bigger than most of the Leggs players. Only Dan, Zoe and Rollo matched up to them. They looked tough too – most of them had close-cropped hair and hard, staring eyes.

When the referee called the two captains for the toss-up, the Weldon Wanderers skipper spat on the grass and strolled to the centre circle. He had very short hair and a gold stud in one ear.

"My name's Paul Starkey," said the ref, offering his hand to Dan. He was a very big man with a smiley face that Dan found reassuring. He looked like a ref who'd be fair and keep good control of the game.

"I'm Dan Legg," Dan replied, shaking the ref's hand.

The ref nodded and turned to the other captain.

"Ricky," growled the Weldon Wanderers leader, barely touching the ref's outstretched hand. His face bore a hostile scowl.

"OK, Ricky, Dan," the ref said amicably, taking a coin from his pocket. "Who's going to call?"

"He can," Ricky muttered with a stiff nod at Dan.

The referee flipped the coin.

"Heads," called Dan.

"Heads it is," said the ref.

"We'll kick off," said Dan. "Which end would you like?" he asked his opposing captain.

"It don't matter," said Ricky. He glanced at the pitch about him as if it were a rubbish dump. "We'll stay where we are," he ventured at last. Then he turned and jogged back to his team.

As Leggs United lined up for the kick-off in their WM formation, Dan was glad he was wearing shin-pads. Somehow he reckoned he was going to need them in this game. Sam wasn't wearing any as usual. Well, that was her lookout. She probably wouldn't get into any tackles anyway, Dan thought, knowing what she was like.

On the touchline, the three sets of parents were together in a group by Archie, who was in his usual match stance – standing near the centre line with one foot on the old ball and his hands on his hips. There was a shimmering aura about him. He looked cool and collected. But, Dan wondered, for how long?

Dan clapped his hands. "Right, Leggs, let's go!" he exhorted. But his call was drowned by a much louder, deeper, harsher shout from the touchline.

"Right, no prisoners, Weldon! Let's get stuck in!"

Looking over in the direction of the cry, Dan saw a burly, bald-headed man in a blue shell-suit. He was standing just a few metres from Archie, who was staring at him now with a slightly baffled air. His attention was quickly diverted back to the pitch, though, when the ref blew his whistle for the game to begin.

It took Weldon Wanderers about five seconds to make their mark. No sooner had Zak kicked the ball to Sam, than Ricky was on to her. She took the ball, looked up to make a pass and *wham!* The Weldon skipper clattered into her with a tackle that left her hopping with pain. But it was a fair tackle, he won the ball

cleanly, and straight away the visitors were on the attack.

Dan was busier in the opening ten minutes of this match than he'd been in the entire game against Downside. Time after time he was called upon to make crucial tackles and interceptions as Weldon Wanderers pressed forward. But after every clearance he made, the ball just came straight back. The visitors were as tough as they looked – they tackled like tigers and harried any Leggs player who had the ball.

Poor Sam couldn't get a kick – well, not of the ball anyway. She got plenty of kicks on her legs. Zak fared no better. Any time the ball came near him he found himself surrounded by big, muscular defenders, who easily shrugged him aside. It was the same story out on the wings with Ben and Frances. With Sam being so tightly marked, they hardly got a chance to run – and when they did it was in vain.

Leggs United were pinned in their own half. Only desperate defending by Dan and the twins, brilliant keeping by Gabby and some very poor shooting by the Weldon forwards prevented the away team from taking a big lead.

As the half went on, the pressure mounted and mounted. Weldon poured forward, winning corner after corner . . .

Finally their pressure told. A third successive corner saw the ball crossed to the far side of the Leggs United six-yard box. Gabby leapt to push the ball away, but the huge Weldon centre half jumped too, towering above her, and nodded the ball into the goal. On the line, Zoe made a brave attempt to stop the ball, but the header was too strong. The ball flew into the net and so did Zoe's glasses. Fortunately, they didn't break.

On the touchline, the Wanderers' coach shook a fist and snarled, "Come on, Weldon! Take them apart now. No prisoners!"

Archie's reaction to these aggressive commands was to give his opposing coach a fizzing stare. "This is a game of football, not a war," he declared indignantly, wagging one bony finger. But, of course, he got no response, for only his own players could see or hear him.

Weldon Wanderers were really fired up now.

The goal and their coach's instructions seemed to make them more competitive than ever. They made full use of their height and weight advantage and their play became even more physical. Some of their challenges drew the displeasure of the referee, but most didn't. When Sam complained about the tackling, the ref just smiled and shook his head.

"Football's a hard game, son," he said airily. Sam glared back at him from under her fringe.

What the referee didn't see were all the nudges, pokes and sly kicks carried out by the Weldon players behind his back. Archie saw, though. He glowered and fumed on the touchline, screaming at the ref to take action. He vented his anger on the Weldon coach and players too.

"Foulers! Dirty cheats! Hooligans!" he cried furiously, as Sam received yet another tap on the shins well away from where the play was.

Finally, Archie could take no more. When Zak was felled by another crunching tackle from the Weldon skipper and the referee waved *Play on*, Archie flared with indignation. But this was nothing compared to his absolute outrage when the move that followed resulted in Weldon Wanderers' second goal – scored by the offending player himself, Ricky.

As the ball hit the back of the Leggs United net, Archie rampaged onto the pitch, glowing as if radioactive. His red hair stood up on end, quivering with electricity.

"Don't you know a foul when you see one!" he shouted angrily at the ref. "Or are you afraid you might wear out your whistle if you blew it?"

At this instant, as if literally adding insult to injury, the referee did indeed blow his whistle. He gave it three loud blasts.

"Half-time!" he announced. Then he trotted away to the side of the pitch, leaving Archie smouldering in his wake.

Chapter Ten
A MINOR RESHUFFLE

At half-time, the Leggs United players sat on the grass and nursed their bruises, while their parents tried to comfort and encourage them. Archie perched on the old ball with his shoulders hunched like a huge sulky eagle.

Julia Browne handed round slices of orange to the team, but she refused to do the same for the visitors – or the referee. Like Archie she was furious about the tackle on Zak that had led to Weldon's second goal.

"It's only a game, Julia," Stephen Legg said, adopting his most soothing doctor's bedside manner.

"Huh," his sister huffed. "That boy could have broken Zak's leg."

Archie nodded vigorously in agreement. "Indeed, he could have," he said. "It was a disgraceful tackle. In my day, it would never have been allowed."

"I thought in your day the game was much tougher," Dan reminded his manager.

"Yes, well, it was," Archie blustered. "Tougher – but fair."

"I've a good mind to have a word with that referee," Julia Browne remarked sharply.

"I'm OK, Mum, really," said Zak hastily – but the marks on his legs told a different tale.

"Now I know why Perry was looking so smug," Dan said ruefully. "He knew what the Wanderers were like."

"I wish I had," winced Sam. "Then I'd definitely have got myself some shin-pads. My left leg is aching all over."

"They are a hard team," Archie conceded grudgingly. "But, I believe, there is a soft centre. We just have to uncover it."

"They certainly keep it well hidden," Sam remarked. She sucked on her orange, wondering gloomily what the second half would bring. If it was more of the same, then she'd rather not play at all – not that she'd ever admit that to Archie, of course. She wasn't going to give him the chance to say all that stuff about football being a man's game. She'd had quite enough of that from the ref. It was all very well for him to talk, she thought bitterly; he was huge. If he was a player, no one would dare to clatter into him.

Archie, meanwhile, was on his feet again. He had a brief, whispered chat with Stephen Legg, who turned and hurried away in the direction of his house. Then the phantom coach came and stood among his players.

"Right," he said, fixing the children with a fiery stare. "I believe I have the solution. There is nothing wrong with the formation we are playing. Defensively we have been excellent, despite the two goals. All that is required is a minor reshuffle."

Archie's reshuffle involved Rollo taking Zak's place as the spearhead of the attack. "We need some extra height and weight up front," he explained. Zak was to drop back and play alongside Sam, with Zoe partnering Jack.

"But how can we get the ball up to Rollo?" Sam grumbled. She gestured at the opposing team. "They just don't give us any time."

Archie raised his hand imperiously. His hairy eyebrows hopped like frisky caterpillars. "Now, now, laddy," he said, and before Sam could correct him he continued, "I've thought of that. Am I not Archibald Legg, master strategist, tactical genius, Herbert Chapman's spiritual heir . . ."

The children groaned.

"Just tell us what you're going to do," said Sam.

Archie glared at her. "I want you and Zak to play further back in your own half," he explained, "behind Zoe and Jack and in front of Dan and the twins, Charles and Martin."

"Giles and Justin!" shrieked the twins as one.

"Mmm, just so," Archie murmured fuzzily. "Zoe and Jack will act as a kind of shield, preventing that hoodlum captain from getting to you and Zak too quickly. You must use the extra time you will have to make your passes count." He looked across pointedly at the whitewash diagram of Arsenal's ten-second wonder goal. "I want to see some goals this half – in *their* net, not ours."

"We'll do our best," Dan said. "Won't we, team?"

"Yes," came the reply, but it didn't sound very convincing.

Sam hobbled to her feet. She grimaced and held out her left leg. "If I get any more kicks on this leg, I reckon it's going to be too sore to play with," she said grimly.

She glanced across at Zak, who was gently rubbing his right leg. "Zak's leg is pretty bad too," she added.

To her surprise, Archie actually looked sympathetic. "Help is at hand, laddy," he said with a small smile.

No sooner had Archie spoken than Stephen Legg appeared with a red face.

"I've got them, Archie," he said breathlessly and he handed over to his ghostly ancestor the ancient pair of bulky shin-guards.

"Just the job," said Archie warmly, clutching the leather guards with affection. He offered

one to Zak and one to Sam. "Put those under the socks on your kicking legs," he instructed.

"But they're huge," Sam protested.

"Precisely," said Archie.

Then, as the referee's whistle blew to summon the teams for the second half, he turned towards the opposition with an icy gaze. "Now we'll see who takes no prisoners," he remarked coolly.

Chapter Eleven
RAISED SPIRITS

Archie's half-time talk had immediate results. Breaking up Weldon Wanderers' first attack, Dan fed the ball to Sam in her new deep position. For once, she found herself in space and with time to look up and consider the situation. She took a couple of strides forward and then whipped a long diagonal pass over the Weldon midfield towards the wing, where Frances was already sprinting forward, leaving her marker behind. The ball dropped perfectly between Frances and the Weldon full-back. Now fully in her stride, the youngest Legg triplet reached the ball well before the defender and was on her way past him before he could adjust to get a tackle in.

It was the first real opportunity Frances had had to run at the Weldon defence in the whole match and she wasn't going to waste it. On and on she raced until she reached the byline, where she chipped a perfect cross into the heart of the Weldon penalty area.

The pace and precision of the move caught the Weldon central defenders napping. Neither of them jumped to cut out the cross and nor did the goalie. It was as if they each expected one of the others to deal with the ball – or maybe, considering how little they'd had to do in the first half, they didn't think there was any danger. But if that was the case, they were wrong.

As the cross arrived at the far post, Rollo flung himself forward and met the ball full on the forehead. It may not have been the most elegant of headers, but it was highly effective. The ball rocketed into the top of the net. Leggs United had struck back with their first attack of the second half.

"Goal!" Stephen Legg cried and he hugged

his sister. The other Legg spectators were just as excited.

"Great header, son!" shouted Otis Browne.

"Let's have another now, Leggs!" Mark Legg called.

On the touchline, the Weldon coach was furious. He shouted and swore and shook his fist at his players, angry with them for their slack defending.

"You dozy bunch of clowns!" he yelled.

Archie, by contrast, remained quite still and seemingly aloof from all the noise and passion around him. But his face betrayed his feelings in the shape of a huge satisfied grin. With its speed, directness and simplicity, the goal had been in the style of the Arsenal ten-second wonder goal itself. Archie had pulled off another tactical master stroke and he knew it.

The goal certainly lifted Leggs United. They played with new vigour and spirit. Protected by Zoe and Jack, Sam and Zak saw a lot more of the ball and were able to display their skills. They raked passes to the wings, dribbled past opponents, and had a couple of shots each.

Meanwhile, up front, Rollo's height and strength gave the visitors plenty to think about. He was the tallest player on the field and they couldn't knock him off the ball as they had Zak. The heading practice he'd done proved very useful too – and not only with the goal. Several times during the half he beat the Weldon defenders in the air to set up good attacking positions for other players. From one of these, Sam rattled the crossbar with a scorching drive.

The match was less tough than in the first half, probably because the Weldon team started to tire, but there was still plenty of rough tackling.

Twice in a matter of minutes, Ben was scythed to the ground by his marker as he set off on a flying run down the wing. Both times, the referee blew for a foul, but he took no further action. He just wagged his finger at the offending player and told him not to do it again.

After the second occasion, however, Archie leapt off his ball in a blazing fury. His face went as red as his hair.

"Take his name, send him off!" he screeched at the ref. "Are you afraid to use your pencil as well as your whistle? What's the matter with you, man?" His anger flared up even more when he heard the Weldon coach applauding his defender.

"You scoundrel!" Archie shouted. "You should be ashamed of yourself." He fizzed with frustration at his inability to make himself heard.

Within a couple of minutes, Weldon Wanderers, in the form of Ricky, committed another blatant foul, this time on Frances. A howl of outrage went up from the Leggs United supporters. The referee blew his whistle and awarded Leggs United a free-kick.

"Keep it clean, son," he said mildly, waving the Weldon skipper away. Ricky turned round with a smirk and spat on the grass – and that was when Archie decided enough was enough.

It was time for him to act.

Chapter Twelve
SUPERGHOST!

One moment Archie was on the touchline, the next he was out on the pitch, fully charged and ready for action.

"What are you doing, Archie?" said Dan, as Archie jogged past him.

"I have come to uphold fair play," Archie replied mysteriously, touching one bony finger to his nose.

Dan shook his head and sighed. Next to him, the Weldon central striker was gaping at Dan as if he thought he was mad. Dan made no attempt to explain why he appeared to be talking to thin air. After all, if he told the truth – that he was talking to a ghost – his opponent would think him even crazier! Besides, Dan was much more interested in what Archie was up to.

He didn't have to wait long to find out. The next time Leggs United went on the attack, Zak lofted another ball over the Weldon midfield into the path of Ben. Once again the middle of the Legg triplets was faced by the Weldon defender who had recently fouled him. Once again, he zipped past him. Once again, the defender's foot went out to bring Ben down . . . Only this time he didn't make contact. Archie nipped in between the two players and tripped the defender up. As Ben ran on, the Weldon player fell over on his backside with a very surprised look on his face.

The next to receive Archie's justice was the Weldon skipper himself. As Sam swerved past him, Ricky moved across to block her and barge her off the ball. Instead of bumping into Sam, though, he found himself colliding with an invisible wall that sent him stumbling backwards. As Sam sprinted on, Ricky stood, gaping with incredulity. "What the . . .?" he muttered, scratching his head.

Archie was everywhere. He was a ghostly dynamo, pulsing with energy. He charged all over the field like a phantom superhero, protecting his players from unfair treatment. He repelled elbow blows, got in the way of ankle-taps, shin-kicks, trips and pushes, and generally flung himself about to prevent foul play.

However, there was a downside to Archie's interventions. The Leggs United players were so mesmerized by his antics that they found it hard to keep their minds on the game. Pass after pass went astray and the few scoring chances they had, they failed to take. Rollo was the main culprit. Scoring goals was not his strength and he missed at least three good chances that Zak would surely have taken. As the match drew to a close, it was still 2–1 to Weldon Wanderers.

Leggs United mounted one last attack down the wing and Ben won a corner. Sam raced over to take the kick. Standing in his own half, Dan glanced across at the touchline and caught sight of Archie's wonder goal diagram. He'd intended to stay where he was in case Weldon got the ball and mounted a counter-attack but, seeing the diagram, he decided to go forward. There was no point in being defensive now. There could only be seconds left. He trotted towards the Weldon penalty area.

Archie, meanwhile, had taken up a position in the middle of the goal ready to rush out and stop any pushes or prods that the Weldon defenders might be planning – particularly on Rollo. They knew that he was the main threat and already three of them had gathered around the tall striker, ready to stop him from getting to the cross that would surely come . . .

But Sam didn't cross the ball. Cleverly, she pushed it out towards Zak, who was standing on the edge of the box unmarked. It was a great ball, but as Zak prepared to shoot, Ricky suddenly slid in to him. The Weldon captain whammed into Zak's leg with a sickening thud. Both players went down.

The ball rolled into the arc of the penalty box just as Dan arrived. Without hesitation, he swung his foot and struck it mightily. It was one of the cleanest shots he'd ever kicked. The ball flew by the crowd of players in the box and

rocketed into the top corner of the Weldon net. The goalie didn't even move. In fact, for an instant, no one moved. Players, spectators, managers – even the referee – seemed in a state of shock.

At last, the referee blew his whistle and a huge cheer went up from the touchline as the Leggs United supporters acclaimed their team's equalizer. But even then Dan didn't celebrate: he was worried about Zak, who was still lying where he had fallen. Dan ran over to his friend.

"Zak," Dan called anxiously. "Are you OK?"

Zak rolled over to face Dan. His large brown eyes sparkled. "I'm fine," he said happily. He nodded at Ricky, who was rolling on the grass nearby, holding his foot and wincing. "I reckon Archie's shin-guard did the trick," Zak laughed and he glanced across at the phantom manager, who was leaning against one of the goalposts, shimmering with satisfaction. Zak turned to Dan once more. "Cool goal," he said admiringly.

"Thanks," said Dan and then, finally, it sank in: the score was 2–2. Leggs United had equalized with the last kick of the match – and it was *his* goal that had saved the day!

Chapter Thirteen
AN HONOURABLE DRAW

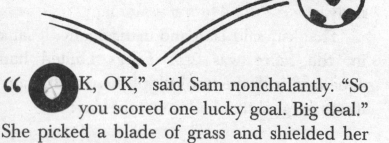

"OK, OK," said Sam nonchalantly. "So you scored one lucky goal. Big deal." She picked a blade of grass and shielded her eyes against the bright morning sun.

"Lucky!" Dan protested. "It was a brilliant strike." He drew back his foot and mimed the shot that had brought the equalizer against Weldon Wanderers the previous afternoon. He kicked so hard that his trainer flew off, sailed through the air and flopped on to the pitch. Sam and Zak laughed as Dan hopped after it. "It *was* a good goal, though, wasn't it?" he said, slipping his trainer back on.

"It was great," Zak assured him. He nodded his head and black ringlets of hair swayed across his eyes.

"It was all right," Sam conceded grudgingly. "It was my corner that set it up, though."

"And my pass," Zak added.

"That wasn't a pass," Sam scoffed, wrinkling her freckly nose. "You were tackled."

"Well, it ended up as a good pass anyway," said Dan. He thought for a moment. "It was a brilliant team effort," he concluded.

"Yeah," Zak agreed. Then he grinned. "I'm glad Archie gave me that shin-guard," he said.

"Me too," said Sam. The eyes of all three children focused on the old ball, lying on the ground in front of them. "Shall I call him?" Sam asked.

Dan nodded. "Go on," he said.

Sam picked up the old ball and went throught her familiar calling-up-Archie routine. She rubbed the ball gently and wailed, "Arise, O Archie. Archie, arise."

The children were expecting the phantom footballer to fizz out of the ball like a

firecracker. But he didn't. What came out was a sort of pale mist.

"Archie?" said Sam questioningly.

And then, at last, Archie did appear, materializing from inside the mist. He was very faint, though – and quite transparent in the bright sunlight. He barely glowed at all.

"Are you all right, Archie?" Dan asked with concern.

Archie's oddly colourless eyebrows met in a deep glare. "Of course I'm not all right," he growled. "You disturbed me from my sleep. I was having a particularly good dream too – I was refereeing the cup final." His eyebrows parted, as his face relaxed into a smile. "I was making an excellent job of it too," he continued, "though I say it myself."

The three children threw back their heads and groaned.

The conversation quickly turned to the match against Weldon. In the end a draw was a good result, they all agreed. At half-time, after all, Leggs United had seemed dead and buried. Archie, however, claimed that the second-half turnaround came as no surprise.

"Let me tell you something particularly wise and original that Herbert Chapman once said on the subject," he pronounced grandly. "He said – and I quote – 'Football is a game of two halves.' " He beamed, inviting appreciation for his hero's brilliance.

The children's reaction, however, was not what Archie expected. They burst out laughing.

"But, Archie," Sam giggled, "that's not original. Everyone says that."

Archie frowned woozily. "Do they?" he muttered. "Well, er, maybe everyone does say that *now*. But Herbert Chapman said it first."

He waggled his walrus moustache emphatically. "Anyway," he went on, "my point is that in the first half of the game, the present, in the shape of Weldon Wanderers, may have come out on top, but in the second, the past and the spirit of the great Herbert Chapman were unquestionably the victors."

"Those old shin-guards certainly came out on top," Zak remarked. "That Ricky was hopping about like he'd kicked a postbox."

Archie tutted with disapproval. "In my day," he sniffed, "that ruffian would not have lasted two minutes. The referee was much too lenient. That's why I had to take matters into my own hands."

"You said you didn't like referees interfering," said Sam pointedly, running her hand over her short red hair.

"Ah, yes, well . . ." Archie appeared flustered for an instant. But he quickly recovered his composure. "When the play is fair, the referee should be invisible," he stated coolly, raising one fuzzy finger. "But when the play is foul, he should intervene and take strong action. That referee failed to do his duty."

"You're right there," said Dan. "That first half was like the Battle of Highbury."

"Indeed," said Archie gravely. "And in a battle, you must have protection. Hence, the shin-guards."

"Yes, well, I've learnt my lesson," said Sam. "I'll wear shin-pads in future. But not those old ones – they were too big. I couldn't play a whole game in *those*."

Archie tutted once more. "As I told you before," he said with a shake of his head, "the great Cliff Bastin managed perfectly well."

"But he was a grown-up!" Sam exclaimed.

"When I first saw him play," sniffed Archie, "he was just a slip of a lad – not much bigger than you."

Sam glanced at Dan and rolled her eyes.

Zak, however, was looking at Archie with real interest. "I've heard of Cliff Bastin," he said brightly.

Archie beamed at his young relative. "Ah, so the legend does endure," he purred.

"He was Arsenal's record goal-scorer," Zak added, showing once again his impressive knowledge of football facts.

"Another victory for the past, it seems," Archie commented smugly.

"Well, not exactly," said Zak and the others all stared at him. "He *was* the record goal-scorer," Zak explained, "but he's not any more. Ian Wright is."

Archie flickered with confusion. "And *who* is Ian Wright?" he boomed.

"He's a player from our day, the present," said Sam with a cheeky grin.

Archie looked deeply perplexed. He seemed fuzzier than ever.

"Well," said Dan, pulling at his ear, "I think football was great in the past and football's great in the present. You can't say which one's better."

Sam and Zak muttered agreement and even Archie nodded his head appreciatively. "Well said, laddy," he murmured. His face relaxed into a warm, hazy smile. "We shall call it an honourable draw . . ."